MONSTER MOUNTAINS

ELF GIRL and RAVEN BOY

MONSTER MOUNTAINS

ELF GIRL and RAVEN BOY

MARCUS SEDGWICK

Illustrated by Pete Williamson

Orion
Children's Books

First published in Great Britain in 2012
by Orion Children's Books
a division of the Orion Publishing Group Ltd
Orion House
5 Upper St Martin's Lane
London WC2H 9EA
An Hachette UK Company

1 3 5 7 9 10 8 6 4 2

A catalogue record for this book is available from the British
Library.

ISBN 978 1 4440 0486 1

Printed and bound by CPI Group (UK) Ltd, Croydon, CR0 4YY

www.orionbooks.co.uk

For Edgar

Scream Sea

The Island

Monster
Mountains

Fright Forest

ONE

Raven Boy is *so* good at climbing trees that he goes higher even than really brave squirrels do.

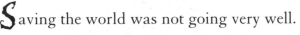

Saving the world was not going very well.

Raven Boy and Elf Girl had left their homeland far behind them, and had been wandering across a wide and empty plain for what seemed like days.

It was, in fact, only an afternoon, but they were already fed up.

Very.

'Look at it!' Raven Boy cried. 'Not a tree in sight!'

'That's what happens when you leave the forest,' Elf Girl said, a little snappily.

'It's your fault,' said Raven Boy. 'You wanted to come this way.'

'Only because it's faster. The other way would have taken five times as long.'

'Yes, but at least there'd have been trees.'

He thought sadly about his favourite pine tree, and wished he could be there, at the top, swaying gently in the breeze.

But Raven Boy knew that Elf Girl was right.

In order to save the world, they'd have to go and find the evil Goblin King, who had sent an ogre to destroy their forest. Having defeated the ogre, they'd learned that the Goblin King lived far away, across the sea. To get to the sea meant a long journey either north or south to get around a huge, dark and gloomy mountain range.

'Although,' the ogre had told them, 'there could be a third way.'

'Which is?' Raven Boy had asked.

'You could go straight over the mountains.

That would be fastest. Only I don't think you'll want to do that.'

Elf Girl hadn't been listening, and there and then had said, 'We'll go the quick way! There's no time to lose!'

And she wouldn't even let Raven Boy stay long enough to find out why going over the mountains might not be a good idea. Just looking at them made Raven Boy nervous.

Since then, they'd hurriedly packed a small bag each, with some food and a hat in case it got cold. After saying goodbye to Elf Girl's family, they'd left. Raven Boy didn't have a family, but he'd spent ages saying goodbye to three owls, a magpie, seventeen sparrows, and giving a badger a hug.

'We've been walking for days,' Elf Girl moaned.

In the far distance, they could see the black mountains, but they never seemed to get any closer.

'It was lunchtime,' muttered Raven Boy.

'What?' asked Elf Girl.

'What what?' asked Raven Boy.

'What was lunchtime?'

'Oh,' said Raven Boy. 'It was lunchtime. When we left.'

'Well, it feels like days.'

'Elf Girl, you'd better get used to it. We've hardly started.'

At that, Rat poked his head out of Raven Boy's pocket, and squeaked.

'I know,' said Raven Boy, tickling Rat's ears.

Elf Girl looked at him suspiciously.

'What?' she said.

'Nothing,' said Raven Boy.

'It can't have been nothing. What did he say?'

'No, nothing, really,' said Raven Boy again.

The ends of Elf Girl's ears started to go pink. Then red.

'What did he say?' she asked, sounding very cross now.

Raven Boy stopped walking and glared at her.

'If you must know, he said, "she does moan a lot, doesn't she?"'

Rat squeaked and quickly disappeared back into Raven Boy's pocket.

'And who did he mean by "she"?' Elf Girl asked. Both her ears were bright red now, but Raven Boy was too cross to care.

'Well, who do you think? There aren't

any other "shes" round here, are there?'

'Well, really!' cried Elf Girl, and with that, she stomped off, heading towards the mountains at double speed.

Rat poked his head out of Raven Boy's pocket again.

He squeaked.

'Yes,' said Raven Boy. 'It's safe now.'

He sighed.

'Come on, we'd better catch up and say sorry.'

They did, and by the time they had, they suddenly realised they'd reached a series of small hills. The ground was rising and falling and a stream babbled beside the path. They stopped for a drink by a stone bridge that crossed the water.

'We're nearly at the mountains,' Raven Boy said when they'd had their drink.

Elf Girl grinned.

'So, whose idea was best then? We'll be over the mountains by tea-time, and then we can get on with finding the Goblin King.'

Raven Boy wasn't so sure about that, and he was just about to say so when he heard something.

'Quick,' he said, 'somebody's coming. Hide under the bridge.'

'Why?' asked Elf Girl.

'In case they're bad people!'

'But they might be good people.'

'In which case hiding under the bridge won't matter. But if they're not good people, and we don't hide under the bridge . . .'

'Ah,' said Elf Girl. 'I see.'

They scrambled down under the bridge as fast as they could.

'Look!' hissed Elf Girl. 'It's the trolls!'

'Those aren't trolls,' whispered Raven Boy. 'They're just three men.'

'Raven Boy! Look! It's the trolls from Fright Forest, only it's daytime. They're in their human form.'

Raven Boy peered harder.

'You're right,' cried Raven Boy. 'Eep!' 'They must be following us.'

They shivered and ducked back out of sight as the three troll-men passed over the bridge.

'I can smell 'em,' said the big one.

'You're just imagining it,' said the middle-sized one.

'Nah, I can smell 'em, I really can.'

'That's the trouble with the daytime,'

said the little one. 'I can always smell better when I'm a proper troll. Not looking like I does in the daytime.'

'Yeah,' said the middle-sized one. 'You're right.'

'But I can still smell 'em,' insisted the big one.

'Look, let's just get on with it, shall we?' said the little one. 'The sooner we catch 'em, the sooner we can boil 'em.'

'And eat 'em?' asked the first voice.

'We're not gonna play chess with 'em, are we?'

At that, all three gave a long, loud and very unpleasant chuckle, and then their footsteps faded away, up the path towards the mountains.

Elf Girl looked at Raven Boy, her eyes wide.

'What are we going to do?' she wailed. 'Hungry trolls ahead of us, and that's just the way we want to go.'

Raven Boy thought carefully about what to say next. Finally he opened his mouth.

'Eep!' he cheeped.

Two

**Before Elf Girl's hut got flattened
by Raven Boy she was planning to
redecorate it with moss green walls
and a sky blue ceiling.**

'If only you knew how to use your bow
properly,' Raven Boy said, 'we could zap those
trolls and be on our way.'

'I do know how to use my bow,' said Elf
Girl. 'Sort of. At least, I got us out of trouble
with it before, didn't I?'

'Yes,' said Raven Boy. Then added quietly,
'By accident . . .'

'Well, I haven't seen you doing anything
deadly or courageous lately.'

'Hang on just a . . .'

Rat stuck his head out of Raven Boy's pocket, and gave the loudest and longest squeak either of them had ever heard.

They both stared at him.

'What did he say?' Elf Girl whispered to Raven Boy.

Raven Boy looked guilty, and sad too.

'He says please can we stop arguing with each other all the time, or he's going home.'

Elf Girl looked sad too.

'Sorry, Rat,' she said.

'Sorry, Rat,' said Raven Boy. 'We will, won't we?'

'Oh yes,' said Elf Girl. 'It's just that it's all so scary and difficult to know what to do.'

'We'll go slowly and keep our eyes and ears open for the first sign of troll trouble.'

'Maybe it would be best to wait until dark.'

'I don't think that would make any difference,' said Raven Boy. 'Didn't you hear? They can smell better in the dark. That means they can probably see and hear better then too. And they'll be hungrier when they're trolls.'

'I don't like it,' said Elf Girl.

'Neither do I,' said Raven Boy, 'but we have no choice. Nobody said saving the world would be easy!'

'Okay, but let's give the trolls a head start. Why don't we count to a thousand, then go?'

So they counted to a thousand. Then, they looked at each other for a second, and counted to a thousand again.

Then they climbed out from under the bridge, and set off up the path.

It wasn't long before the hills turned into the foot of the mountains, and not much longer after that that they came to a sign by the path.

STOP, it said.

STOP!
TURN ROUND
AND GO
BACK

They didn't.

A little further on, they found another sign.

DIDN'T YOU READ THE SIGN? it said. **GO BACK. AHEAD LIE THE MONSTER MOUNTAINS.**

'The Monster Mountains?!' cried Elf Girl. 'That doesn't sound too wonderful.'

'**E**EP!' cried Raven Boy, but they both took a deep breath and walked on.

Soon, they came to a third sign.

THREE

Trolls are not only mean and vicious
and smelly, they also never brush
their teeth and their tongues are
yellow and slimy.

'Raven Boy,' said Elf Girl, 'Do you
think we . . .'

'No,' said Raven Boy. 'We've come too
far this way now. We have to go on. Anyway,
we're two very small and tiny people. And a
rat. No one's going to take any notice of us,
are they?'

Elf Girl didn't look sure, but Raven Boy
was right. It was too late to go back.

The path began to climb steeply into the mountains. The landscape around them was bleak and rocky, and they heard nothing, not even a single bird in the sky.

'Do . . . do you think there really are monsters in these mountains?' asked Elf Girl.

'No,' said Raven Boy, as they rounded a corner. 'Look!'

He began to laugh.

'That's probably the kind of thing they mean!'

In front of them stood a goat.

It was standing right in the middle of the path, facing them.

Raven Boy laughed some more.

The goat looked at them. It had a short beard and two very long curly horns on its head. It didn't look pleased to see them.

Raven Boy laughed.

'Look, it's just a silly old goat.'

A second later, the goat charged at him, and Raven Boy was hurtling back down the path as fast as he could. It wasn't fast enough.

The goat rammed him from behind and he ended up head first in a bush. Elf Girl ran up to find him rubbing his bottom.

'Ow,' he said, grumpily. 'That really hurt.'

Elf Girl began to laugh.

'You look so serious,' she said.

'You don't want to do that . . . !' shouted Raven Boy, but before Elf Girl could ask why, she'd joined him in the bush, and there was the goat, his horns still wobbling from butting Elf Girl on the behind.

'Ow,' she said.

'I don't think it likes people laughing,' said Raven Boy.

The goat had returned to its place in the middle of the path, a short way ahead. It glared at them and didn't look as if it was going to move any time soon.

'I'll try again. But no laughing this time.'

Raven Boy walked towards the goat, putting on the most serious face he could.

'Good evening, Mr Goat,' he said, and was about to walk casually past it.

A moment later and he was back in the
bush, rubbing his bottom again.

'Ow,' he said.

'I think,' said Elf Girl, 'he just doesn't
like people at all. Why don't you try talking
to him?'

Raven Boy stood up.

'Okay. But he doesn't look very chatty,

you know.'

Elf Girl watched as Raven Boy approached the goat again. He stopped a good way off and she could see that he was talking to it. He spoke for a long time, and then finally the goat gave one loud and very short bleat.

Raven Boy turned around and stomped back to Elf Girl.

'Of all the rude, insulting, horrible, mean . . .'

'What is it?' asked Elf Girl. 'Won't he let us past?'

'No,' said Raven Boy, glaring behind him. 'And not only that, he said some very rude things about us.'

'He did?'

'Yes, he did.'

'Like what?'

'You don't want to know.'

'I do want to know, Raven Boy,' Elf Girl said, 'That's why I'm asking.'

Raven Boy could see her ears turning pink again, and at the risk of upsetting Rat, he took a deep breath.

'Well, he called me scruffy, and he said you have silly ears.'

'That does it!' cried Elf Girl. 'No one makes fun of my ears.'

She jumped out of the bush, pulling her bow from the top of her bag.

She ran forward and aimed at the goat, who lowered his horns and began to charge.

Raven Boy marvelled as from nowhere, a magical string appeared on her bow, and glowed brightly. Elf Girl let fly.

There was a blinding flash of light and when it cleared, there was nothing left of the goat at all. Just a small puff of smoke, and the smell of burning hair.

'Elf Girl! You actually did it. No flowers, no bumble bees! No blocks of ice! You actually did something deadly with your bow! Hooray!'

Elf Girl laughed nervously.

'I did, didn't I?'

'That's fantastic. I feel much safer now,' cried Raven Boy. He laughed. 'Silly trolls! They don't stand a chance.'

Elf Girl smiled, a little feebly.

Raven Boy looked at her. 'What is it? You . . . You do know how you did it, don't you?'

Elf Girl shook her head.

'No,' she said, 'it just happened. I haven't the slightest idea how.'

Raven Boy swallowed hard.

'At least,' he said, 'we know you can do something deadly, yes? Now all you have to do is work out how to do it again. That can't be too hard, can it?'

'No,' agreed Elf Girl, looking happier. 'That can't be too hard.'

As night fell they found an old stone shack to sleep in, where they thought they'd be a bit safer. They were both very quiet indeed, and Rat didn't even poke his head out to say goodnight.

FOUR

Raven Boy has never cut his hair so it's always a bit of a mess, but he has no idea why he keeps finding feathers in it.

Raven Boy and Elf Girl had a bad night's sleep, mostly because they were still sore from where the goat had biffed them, and every time they turned onto their backs it hurt so much they woke up.

By dawn, they were wide awake.

'Raven Boy,' Elf Girl said, 'I've been thinking.'

'So have I,' Raven Boy said. 'What have you been thinking?'

'I've been wondering where the trolls are. And whether they got past the goat. If they didn't, that must mean they've gone a different way, so maybe we've lost them.'

'Maybe,' agreed Raven Boy. 'But maybe they just went past it. They're bigger and tougher than us.'

'But in that case, they'd have probably eaten it, wouldn't they?'

Raven Boy thought about this.

'So, anyway,' Elf Girl went on. 'What have you been thinking?'

'Well,' said Raven Boy, 'I've been wondering how your bow works.'

'Yes, I've been thinking that too.'

'Did you say anything, or think anything, when you fired at the goat? Something different from when you used it in Fright Forest?'

'Like with the flowers, and the bees?'

Raven Boy nodded.

'Yes. But also, I never told you, when you fired at the ogre, and put him to sleep, the arrow mark on your arm began to glow.'

'It did what?'

Elf Girl looked doubtful, but Raven Boy nodded again.

'Yes, the arrow-shaped birthmark on your arm. It glowed like the bowstring does when you fire it. It glowed again when you fired at the goat. So, did you do anything differently?'

'I don't think so. I was just really cross.'

'Maybe that's it,' said Raven Boy. 'You have to be cross to use it.'

'Maybe,' said Elf Girl. 'That doesn't seem right though. My mum never used to be cross when she used it. And she did all sorts of things with it.'

'But she also said it's different for everyone who uses it, didn't she? So maybe *you* have to be cross.'

'Well, that would be awkward, wouldn't it? I'm not cross that much, am I?'

Raven Boy rolled his eyes.

'Am I? Raven Boy! Am I?'

'No, no,' he said

quickly. 'You're not. But I could always stamp on your toes if you need to use it.'

Elf Girl looked hard at Raven Boy.

'I'm not sure that's very helpful, actually.'

'Sorry,' said Raven Boy.

'Raven Boy?' asked Elf Girl.

'Yes, what is it?'

'I've been thinking something else.'

'What's that?'

'Supposing we've been very stupid,' she said.

'What do you mean?'

'I mean, supposing we've been stupid. Supposing we made a stupid decision, to go and save the world, I mean. The Goblin King sounds scary, and strong. And really, really mean. He made that ogre rip up our forest! Someone who can control an ogre like that . . . How are we going to defeat him?'

Raven Boy nodded thoughtfully.

'I was thinking the same thing,' he said.

Just then, Rat woke up and saw them both looking glum.

He squeaked at Raven Boy.

'What did he say?' asked Elf Girl.

Raven Boy swallowed.

'Rat said he's been thinking that he's scared but then he woke up and saw us and he knows how brave we are and now he doesn't feel scared any more so shall we get on with finding the Goblin King so everyone can sleep safely in their beds?'

'He said all that with a squeak?' asked Elf Girl.

Raven Boy nodded.

'In that case,' said Elf Girl, 'we'd better get on with it.'

'Yes,' agreed Raven Boy, 'We'd better.'

FIVE

The Monster Mountains are so high there's always snow on them, even in summer.

The mountains towered above them as they wove their way up the path, which twisted this way and that. With every step they were getting higher and higher, and though it was a clear and sunny day, it began to get icy cold.

The rocks around them began to turn into all sorts of strange shapes. Raven Boy thought they looked like monsters themselves, with spiny backs and long teeth.

They heard noises, slithering and sliding sounds of things moving nearby, always just out of sight, and once, they heard a rumbling roar in the distance. A huge, long growl that echoed all around the valley walls.

'E EP!' said Raven Boy.

The higher they got, the further they could see.

'Wow,' said Elf Girl. 'That's home, isn't it?'

In the distance, sprawled Fright Forest, and beyond it, their own patch of woodland. Or what was left of it.

'**Eep!**' cried Raven Boy. 'Look how much damage that ogre did! There are so many trees missing!'

Elf Girl pushed her blonde hair back behind her ears, looking determined. 'That Goblin King has a lot to answer for when we find him.'

She spoke loudly, trying to sound brave, but she didn't actually feel that brave. Especially as she was sure she'd just seen the tail of something nasty slink off behind a rock.

She would have given almost anything to be at home in her little hut in the woods with her family. Except that she didn't have a little hut any more; it had been squashed flat by one of the trees the ogre had uprooted.

'Raven Boy?' asked Elf Girl.

'Yes, what is it?'

'What is it you say? When you're sad? You know

what I mean . . . What is it?'

'Oh,' said Raven Boy. 'You mean "meep".'

'Yes, that's it,' said Elf Girl. 'Well, meep.'

Raven Boy was about to say how meepish he was feeling too, when Rat poked his head out from a pocket and gave a tiny squeak.

Raven Boy sighed.

'Come on, there's no use looking back. We have to get along.'

'It's so cold!' moaned Elf Girl, but they set off again, up the mountain, step by step.

'Are you sure you know where we're going?' asked Elf Girl.

'No,' said Raven Boy. 'Only we have to go up to get over the mountains, don't we? So that means going up. And when we can't go up any more, it will be time to go down again, right?'

'Er, I think so,' said Elf Girl. There was something she couldn't quite understand about Raven Boy's plan, which was that perhaps they didn't have to go to the very top of the very highest mountain to get to the other side, but her brain was too cold to work it out at that moment.

Once more, the sound of slithering came from the rocks around them, a noise like claws scraping on stone. Something hissed and for a second Elf Girl thought she felt hot breath on her neck, but when she turned round, nothing was there.

They stopped to eat their lunch. It was a cold potato cake, which Elf Girl's mother had made. It was the last one.

When they'd finished, Raven Boy felt worried. They hadn't brought that much food with them, and he was starting to wonder if their journey was going to be a much longer one than they'd planned for.

But he said nothing to Elf Girl, because he didn't want to worry her too.

The trouble was, there was nothing to eat on the mountain. It was bare and empty, or so it seemed, not like the forest, which was full of life, and full of nuts and berries and honey and other yummy things to eat.

As they moved on, there were more of those strange rocks that looked like animals, but this time Raven Boy was sure they really were.

'Elf Girl,' he said, 'Do those look like monsters to you?'

'They're stone,' she said.

'I know,' Raven Boy said, 'but they look like they were monsters once. Look at that one!'

He pointed at a large rock that looked just like a dragon, with wings, and claws, and teeth. And then at another one that appeared to be a huge, fat snake with long fangs.

'You have a crazy imagination,' said Elf Girl, and she walked on, leaving Raven Boy staring at the rock a while longer.

Then, it began to snow.

It was gentle at first, big soft snowflakes that drifted in the breeze, twisting and spinning, and it cheered them up to see how pretty it was, even though it was freezing.

Pretty soon, there was a lot of snow underfoot, and Raven Boy scooped up a handful to make a snowball, which he threw at Elf Girl.

Elf Girl's ears went pink, and she looked cross, but only briefly, because then she grabbed a big handful of snow and chucked it at Raven Boy, catching him on the back of the head as he ran away.

Throwing snowballs, diving and ducking, they went higher and higher into the hills, until the path vanished beneath the snow.

'How do we know where to go?' asked Elf Girl, but she already knew what Raven Boy was going to say.

'Up!' he said. 'Always up.'

The snow started to fall harder and faster, and it got windy. In no time at all, the wind was so fierce that the snow was whirling in front of their faces, making it almost impossible to know which way was up and which was down, but they kept going, little by little, trying to catch sight of the mountains when they could.

'My feet are cold!' cried Raven Boy.

'So are my hands!' added Elf Girl. 'Why did we play snowballs? That was stupid.'

Their hair was covered in snowflakes, and their shoulders, and even Rat had snow on his whiskers, and soon disappeared inside Raven Boy's pocket. Raven Boy could feel him shivering through the lining of his coat, and wished he could climb into somebody's pocket too.

'At least,' he said to Elf Girl. 'At least we haven't seen any monsters. That sign was silly. We haven't seen anything scary at all.'

'Except that goat,' said Elf Girl.

'And you soon dealt with him! Pow!' cried Raven Boy. 'One zap with your magic bow and . . . pow!'

He pretended he was Elf Girl, aiming her magic bow, anything to take his mind off

the cold and the snow, and then he walked slap
bang into Elf Girl, who was standing and staring
at something on the ground.

'Er,' she said, 'You know what you
were just saying? About monsters? I think you
should look at this . . .'

She pointed at the snow in front of what
she could see of her pointy boots, where there
was a giant footprint.

It was about as long as four of their footprints put together, and had sharp pointy claw marks at the end of each toe.

'Oh golly,' whispered Elf Girl.

'Monsters!' moaned Raven Boy.

'Monsters from Monster Mountains! EEP!'

SIX

**Elf Girl wishes her mum had given
her her magic bow a lot sooner so
she'd had time to work out how
to use its magic.**

Shivering like jellies from cold and fear,
they stared at the footprint in the snow.

'Look!' cried Elf Girl. 'Here's another!'

She stood by a second footprint, and they
could see from the big toe that it was the other
foot this time.

'Holy wow,' said Elf Girl in a very small
voice. 'Look how long its stride is!'

She was, as so often, right. The beast

could have stepped over a small house, or at
least a large hut.

'Raven Boy,' she said, 'I don't like this
one little bit.'

'Nor me,' he agreed. 'Let's find somewhere
to shelter tonight, or we'll freeze to death. Never
mind the monster.'

It was hard to tell with the snow falling
so thickly, but it was definitely getting dark,
and they were surrounded by a wide and tall
emptiness of snow.

Suddenly, the wind dropped to nothing
and the snow stopped falling.

'Crumbs,' said Raven Boy. 'Look.'

It was a beautiful sight. The mountains
were covered in deep soft white snow, and the
sun was sinking behind them. It was still and
quiet.

'Look how high up we are,' said Elf Girl,
and even Rat scurried onto Raven Boy's shoulder
to get a better view.

He squeaked.

'He means wow,' said Raven Boy.
'Yes, I think I got it,' she said, laughing.

'Raven Boy . . .?' she asked. 'What's that?'

She pointed way above their heads, to where the mountain rose above them like a cliff face. Way up, way, way up, she'd seen something.

'It looks like a building of some kind, doesn't it?'

'Maybe,' said Raven Boy. 'It could just be a cliff face, couldn't it? A smooth rock or something? It's so far away.'

'Yes,' said Elf Girl. 'Do you think we

should head for it? Will we make it before dark?'

Raven Boy didn't answer.

'Raven Boy?' asked Elf Girl, turning to him, but he wasn't there.

She whirled about, but sure enough, Raven Boy had vanished into thin air. Which was precisely where he was.

He screamed, and Elf Girl looked up to see him dangling from the claws of some kind of flying monster. It was like an eagle but covered in scales, and it was as ugly as a troll's bottom.

'Help!' Raven Boy cried.

Elf Girl shrieked.

'Raven Boy! What are you doing up there?'

'What do you think I'm doing!' wailed Raven Boy. 'Get me down!'

'I'll use my bow,' said Elf Girl, whipping it from her shoulder.

'Nooo!' screamed Raven Boy. 'You'll turn me into toast like you did that poor goat!'

'What shall I do then?' shouted Elf Girl, frantically.

The flying beast was having trouble
getting much height, and was whirling above
Elf Girl's head.

Suddenly, she had an idea. She rummaged in the snow, and although it was quite deep, she found what she was looking for.

A rock, about the size of her fist.

'Nooo!' Raven Boy screamed again, but Elf Girl took no notice.

'Catch!' she yelled, throwing the rock up into the air, so that Raven Boy was able to catch it neatly.

'Now what?' he wailed. 'Do I brain the thing?'

'No! Put it in your pocket!'

Raven Boy didn't understand, but he did as he was told, as Elf Girl threw rock, after rock, after rock. Raven Boy put them all in his pockets.

Rat was not amused, and scampered onto Raven Boy's head, digging his claws into Raven Boy's hair, holding tight.

With each rock that Raven Boy caught, he was getting a little heavier and the giant beast, strong though he was, was tiring.

'Elf Girl! You're a genius!' cried Raven Boy, as he got lower and lower to the ground.

It seemed that the monster had had enough. It dropped Raven Boy, and he landed in the soft snow, laughing.

'Are you okay, Rat?' he asked, and Rat squeaked.

'Let's get out of here quickly,' cried Elf Girl, 'before he comes back with his friends.'

So they did, running without knowing where to go, and without looking either.

They were more worried about the flying nasty zooming back than they were about seeing where they were going. Suddenly, Rat gave a great squeak, and they both realised at the same moment that they were about to run over the edge of a steep drop.

Too late!

A split second later, they were falling and sliding down a snow-covered slope, hurtling who knows where.

SEVEN

The monsters in Monster Mountains all used to meet (except for the Yetis) for a full-moon howl until so many of them got turned to stone they can only meet for a full-moon whimper.

At some other time, sliding down a snowy slope might have been fun. But not when it's nearly dark, the slope is very steep and you have no way of knowing where you're going to end up.

So when Raven Boy and Elf Girl screamed, 'Eeeeeeeee!' it wasn't from fun, but from fear.

They seemed to slide forever, tumbling
and slipping, and a short way away, Rat was
sliding too, trying to dig his sharp claws into the
snow like ice brakes.

'Elllllf Giiiiiirl!' Raven Boy wailed.
'Raaaaaaa-ven Boooooy!'

'Squeeeeeak!'

And then, with a swoop, they flew
through the air, and landed with a bump in a
deep pile of snow.

Raven Boy pawed his way out and
looked for Elf Girl.

All he could see were two feet in pointy
boots poking up from the snowdrift.

'Elf Girl?' he called.

There was no reply, but he studied her
ankles for a moment, then grabbed them and
yanked hard.

Elf Girl landed on top of him with a yell.

'Ow!' she said. Then, 'Where are we?'

'I don't know.'

They were in some sort of clearing, like a
miniature valley, with low cliffs all around and
only one way in.

Strangely there was a camp fire lit in the middle of the clearing, and they were both glad to see it.

They ran over to it and practically roasted themselves on the spot.

'Oooh, I never thought I'd be warm again,' said Elf Girl.

'Nor me,' Raven Boy agreed. 'Hey! Where's Rat?'

Raven Boy felt in all his pockets and then he remembered.

'He was on my head when we ran.'

'He must have fallen off,' said Elf Girl.

'So where is he?'

They hunted around where they'd landed, calling Rat, but hearing no reply. They dug through the snow, almost afraid to find him in case something awful had happened. But there was no sign of him at all.

Eventually, freezing all over again, they had to go back to the fire to get warm.

There was a stack of logs nearby and Raven Boy plonked a couple onto the flames, sending sparks shooting into the night sky.

'Are you sure that's a good idea?' asked Elf Girl.

'Maybe not, but it's that or freeze to death,' said Raven Boy. 'We don't have much choice.'

'No,' agreed Elf Girl. 'I suppose not. Whose fire do you think this is, anyway? Don't you think it's odd to find a fire burning with no one looking after it?'

'Well, yes,' said Raven Boy, 'but I'm sure there's a reason for it, and you know, whoever it is, they're almost bound to be friendly. It's probably someone who's lost, like us.'

'Friendly?' gasped Elf Girl. 'Sometimes, Raven Boy, I swear you're as stupid as you look.'

At that moment, the owners of the camp fire staggered back into camp, carrying another load of wood.

'Oh, look,' said the big troll.

'Heh, heh, heh,' said the middle-sized troll.

'And there was you two sayin' we had nuffin' to eat,' said the little troll.

'Oh no,' said Raven Boy and Elf Girl at the same time.

It was too late to do anything, even run. The three trolls were blocking the only way in and out, and the sides of the little valley were like walls of ice.

'Oh, nuts,' said Raven Boy.

'Now,' said the little troll, 'Nuts would be nice, and some cabbage and gravy, but you'll just have to do as you are.'

'Not if I can help it!' cried Elf Girl, reaching for her pack and her bow. It wasn't there. Neither the pack, nor the bow.

'Oh, sausages,' she said.

'That would be nice too, but we take what we're given, don't we, boys?'

The other two trolls laughed, in a mean, nasty troll kind of way.

'You're not going to eat us, are you?' said Elf Girl.

'Oh no,' said the little troll. 'We're hungry man-eatin' trolls, and we're not gonna eat you!'

'Aren't we?' asked the big troll. He looked very disappointed.

The little troll turned to the big troll, and rolled his eyes.

'Of course we're gonna eat them!' he shouted. 'I was bein' sarcastic, obviously.'

'What's sar-car-stic?' asked the middle-sized troll.

The little troll rolled his eyes again.

'It's where you say sumfin' that isn't true.'

'Why?' asked the big troll.

'Because it's funny,' said the little troll, getting rather cross.

The big troll blinked a couple of times.

'Why?' he asked.

'It just is! Okay?' screeched the little troll, just as the middle-sized troll pointed at Elf Girl and Raven Boy, who had tried to sneak off while they were arguing.

'Stop 'em!'

'Oh, nuts,' said Raven Boy again, as the trolls jumped in front of them.

'Not so easy as that, eh?' said the little troll. 'And now, if you please, you can get on that fire and roast yourselves.'

The big troll was jumping up and down with excitement, prodding the middle-sized troll with a fat finger.

'Didn't I say I could smell 'em? Didn't I? When we was out gettin' firewood, didn't I say that?'

The middle-sized troll gave the big troll a whack.

'Stop pokin' me and help me get 'em on the fire, will ya?'

'Right,' said the big troll. 'Right.'

'Okay,' said the little troll to Raven Boy and Elf Girl. 'Get yer clothes off and get on the fire.'

'I'm not taking my clothes off!' cried Elf Girl. She sounded like she meant it.

'Why not?' asked the little troll.

'It's cold, for one thing.'

'Yer about to get on a stinkin' fire,' said the little troll, rolling his eyes again.

'I don't care, I'm not doing it,' said Elf Girl.

'Right. Fine,' said the little troll. 'We'll roast you in your jackets.'

'Like potatoes,' said the middle-sized troll, sniggering.

'Huh, yeah. Potatoes,' said the big one.

'So then,' said the little troll. 'Who's going first?'

EIGHT

Trolls can't really help being horrible; it's an important part of their job.

'Oh, Raven Boy,' said Elf Girl. 'I really don't want to be eaten.'

'Meep,' said Raven Boy. 'Nor do I. At least Rat got away somewhere. Maybe he can go home and tell everyone what happened to us.'

'But Raven Boy, you're the only one who can understand what animals say. No one will know.'

'Meep,' he said, sadly.

'Awww, that's really touchin' an' everythin',' said the little troll, 'but would you please get on the fire now! We're hungry!'

Raven Boy looked at Elf Girl, and Elf Girl looked at Raven Boy, and neither of them said anything.

'Now!' screeched the little troll, and Raven Boy sighed.

'Oh, well,' he said, 'Come on then, Elf Girl. It was nice knowing you.'

They took a step towards the fire, and at least they felt warmer for a moment. Very soon, however, they would be too warm. Much too warm.

Raven Boy stopped.

'Can you hear something rumbling?' he said.

'Yeah, my tummy,' growled the big troll. 'Get! On! The! Fire!'

'No, really,' said Raven Boy, 'I can hear something rumbling.'

'I can hear it too,' cried Elf Girl. 'Up there.'

Now everyone heard it. Way above their heads, there was a loud rumbling, roaring noise, and it was getting louder.

'What the piggin' . . .?' said the little troll.

'It's an avalanche!' screamed Raven Boy. 'Run!'

'What's a vala-hanch?' mumbled the big troll.

'Lorks! He's right,' cried the middle-sized troll, and he began to run around in circles, then smacked into the other two.

Raven Boy and Elf Girl didn't waste any time. The rumbling was getting louder and louder. It sounded like a thunder cloud heading right for them.

'Run, Elf Girl, run!'

She ran, and Raven Boy followed her, out of the little valley, and onto the mountainside again. As they ran, they turned and were just in time to see the first wave of the avalanche hit the trolls in a massive wall of snow, sweeping them away in a second.

'Don't stop!' cried Elf Girl. 'There's more!'

Raven Boy was not about to stop.

'Quick!' he cried.

They ran into the dark, hearing the power of the snowfall behind them.

'Look!' yelled Raven Boy. 'In there!'

Ahead was the entrance to a small cave.

'Get inside!'

They threw themselves into the cave, just as the avalanche smashed down overhead.

They spun round and sat watching the snow and ice hammering down past the cave mouth. It was black outside with only a pale moon and starlight to show anything at all. As they sat in the cave, it got darker and darker and gradually, as they were plunged into total darkness, they realised what had happened.

The avalanche had blocked them in.

'Oh,' said Raven Boy in a small voice.

They listened for a long time as the snow kept crashing down outside, and the whole cave seemed to shake.

Finally, it stopped.

'What are we going to do?' asked Elf Girl.

'Wait here,' said Raven Boy.

He felt his way forwards to where the cave mouth had been until he reached the snowfall, and scraped the fallen snow with his bare hands.

'It's as hard as rock,' he said. 'The ice is solid. We're not going to get out that way. Well, not until springtime . . .'

'But Raven Boy, by then, we'll be very skinny . . .'

'EEP!' said Raven Boy. 'What are we going to do?'

'I don't know,' whispered Elf Girl. 'I don't have the faintest idea.'

Raven Boy crawled back to Elf Girl, bumping into her.

'Ow,' she said.

'Sorry. It's kind of hard to see. In fact, impossible.'

'It's okay,' said Elf Girl.

'But it's not okay. We're stuck in here and Rat is out there somewhere. You've lost your bow and that's the one thing that might have got us out of here. You could have zapped the ice. Or made some light with the glowing string. Hey! Do you think you can make your arrow glow, on your arm?'

'No,' she said. 'I don't think I can.'

'Wait!' said Raven Boy. 'Did you hear something?'

'No . . .' said Elf Girl. But her nose began to twitch. 'But I can smell something.'

'Ooh, uck,' said Raven Boy. 'Yes, you're right. But listen, can't you hear those footsteps?'

They both froze even more than they were already frozen as they heard the sound of shuffling, heavy footsteps coming closer.

Then, there was a roar and they both jumped to their feet.

'Maybe this isn't a cave!' cried Raven Boy. 'Maybe it's a tunnel!'

'And there's something here!' wailed Elf Girl. 'A monster!'

'Run!' they both cried together. Too late.

From the darkness, two huge hairy paws swept down, plucked them into the air by the scruff of their necks, and they both fainted.

NINE

There are hundreds of ice tunnels in
Monster Mountains; all dug by the
Yetis who like to stay underground
in the freezing cold.

When Raven Boy and Elf Girl woke up
again, they were still swinging along in the air,
one in each paw of a huge hairy beast.

There was some light now, and they
could not only see each other from time to time
as they swung along in the monster's grasp, but
also the tunnels around them, which were made
of ice.

'Elf Girl!' whispered Raven Boy, afraid
the monster would hear.

'What?' she whispered back.

'Where are we? Where's he taking us?'

'I don't know, Raven Boy. But the tunnels are made of ice, I just saw the sky through one bit. It's daylight. He must have been walking for ages.'

'I suppose we're somewhere up in the mountains. What are we going to do?'

'Shh!' whispered Elf Girl. 'He's stopping.'

They had reached a large ice cave. A gentle light filtered down from above, though the walls seemed to be dark, as if there was solid stone behind the snow.

The beast dropped Raven Boy and Elf Girl on the floor, and stood back to look at them.

Raven Boy and Elf Girl screamed.

The monster was enormous. In fact, he was bigger than enormous. He was like a walking oak tree. His head had scraped the roof of the tunnel, and he still looked big in the huge cave. He was covered from head to foot in long white shaggy hair. The only other things to be seen were the huge claws on his paws, and his mouth, which he opened to roar at them.

It was so loud they stopped screaming.

'Your breath smells,' said Raven Boy to
the monster.

'Is it any wonder?' cried Elf Girl. 'Look!'

She pointed to the edges of the cave,
where there were piles of bones.

'Do they look like people bones to you?'
she asked. 'Raven Boy, can't you talk to him?
Ask him not to eat us, please!'

'I can't. I'm trying but I can't hear much in his head. It's as if his brain is made of fur and there's only one thing on his mind.'

'Which is?'

'He's saying one thing. Eat them, eat them, eat them . . .'

'Ah,' said Elf Girl, and they both screamed again.

The monster roared, and snatched Elf Girl up in the air. He opened his mouth, which was not only like a cave, but was lined with long razor-sharp teeth. Elf Girl dangled above his open jaws, and it looked as though he was about to pop her in his mouth in one gulp.

Raven Boy jumped to his feet and charged at the monster, but he didn't even reach its knees, and when he tried to kick its ankle, all he found was deep, deep fur.

'Noooo!' wailed Elf Girl.

'Why,' shouted Raven Boy, 'does everyone want to eat us?'

'That's a good question, my boy,' said a quiet voice behind him.

Raven Boy turned to see a funny-looking

little man in a long red gown, looking up at the monster. He had a long grey beard, but almost no hair on the top of his head.

'Naughty,' he said, and pulled a short, thin wooden stick from somewhere inside the red gown.

He pointed at the beast.

'Put her down,' he said.

The monster froze, but kept Elf Girl dangling above his slimy open jaws.

'Put her down now,' said the man again, and the monster made a growling noise, and dribbled. To Raven Boy it sounded as if he was complaining.

'I'm not telling you again,' said the man, and waggled the stick at the monster.

A bolt of lightning shot out of the end and scorched the monster's hair with a jet of blue flame.

The beast roared, and dropped Elf Girl, who landed with a bump. Raven Boy ran over to her.

'I'm okay,' she said, getting to her feet.

They turned to see the man aim another zap of lightning at the monster, who went and sat down in a corner of the cave.

It looked very much as though he was sulking.

The man turned to Raven Boy and Elf Girl.

'Well, well,' he said. 'All ready? Good. Come on then.'

He began to wander out of the cave through a smaller tunnel, one too low for the monster to be able to follow, even if he wasn't afraid of being zapped again.

Elf Girl and Raven Boy looked at each other as the man disappeared, and, with a nod, they hurried after him.

'Ah, there you are,' the man said as they caught up. 'Good. You see, I thought I heard some screaming, and to be honest I knew that

the yeti would be behind it all. Thought I'd
better come and have a look, because I know
what he's like. Always eating someone. Given
half a chance.'

He prattled on and on, as if he would
never stop talking, but when he paused for
breath, Raven Boy managed to ask, 'That thing
was a yeti?'

'Oh, yes, a yeti,' said the man. He wasn't
even as tall as Raven Boy, and yet he'd been
powerful enough to scare the yeti into letting
them go.

'And is that thing you used a magic wand?'

'A wand?' asked the man. 'Oh, yes, a
wand. It's a wand, isn't it? I wouldn't be much
of a wizard if I didn't have a magic wand.
Would I?'

'A wizard!' Raven Boy and Elf Girl
whispered.

They stared at each other, goggle-eyed
and open-mouthed.

'Eep!' said Raven Boy.

TEN

There are lots of Yetis in the mountains, but they all live alone, because they're so bad-tempered, especially when they bump into each other by mistake in the ice tunnels.

Raven Boy and Elf Girl hurried along after the wizard, who, though very short, could move very quickly.

They were climbing up through the mountain now and were back in tunnels made of stone. Once again, there seemed to be stone creatures all around them; things with claws and things with wings, and some things with claws *and* wings, but the wizard took no notice of them.

He waved his wand and it gave off a
bright glow, so they could see their way, but
Raven Boy got the feeling the wizard could
have made the journey blindfolded, because
he didn't pause once, just kept on walking and
chatting all sorts of nonsense.

'A wizard needs a wand,' he was saying. 'Very useful against yetis, of course, but all sorts of other things too. All sorts of beasties, you know. Of course it can't do everything, but there you are. One does one's best. Ah! Here we are!'

They'd come to a small door in the rock. The wizard fumbled inside his robe and brought out a large key, with which he unlocked the door.

He stood aside and Raven Boy and Elf Girl hurried through. The wizard joined them, shutting the door behind them, and locking it again.

'There we are, no more yetis today, eh? Come along!'

He shuffled off, along a long narrow passageway, which opened into a hall, and they saw they were inside a castle.

'This must be what we saw from the base of the cliff!' said Elf Girl.

'You were right,' agreed Raven Boy. 'Thank my beak it's a little warmer in here.'

'Come along, come along,' the wizard called, impatiently. 'All sorts of things to do,

I have stuff to get ready and there are never enough hours in the day, are there?'

'Couldn't you make some more?' asked Elf Girl.

'What what?' said the wizard.

'I mean, couldn't you make some more hours in the day?'

The wizard thought about this for a moment.

'I'm a wizard, not a miracle worker. I can't do just anything. Now, do come along, you'll be wanting to see your room and I have lots to do. Lots. Follow me.'

Elf Girl raised her eyebrows at Raven Boy, who just shrugged.

'So he's a bit odd,' he whispered. 'It's better than being eaten by a yeti.'

They followed him through the corridors of the castle: they crossed huge halls and ballrooms, teetered over narrow bridges above bottomless drops, walked around parapets and must have seen a hundred suits of armour but, amazing though the wizard's castle was, Raven Boy was worrying about something else.

'Excuse me,' he said, trying to catch the wizard's attention.

The wizard seemed not to have heard and was chattering away about all the things he had to do.

Raven Boy tried again, tugging the wizard's sleeve.

'Yes, what what?' asked the wizard, irritated to have been interrupted.

'Oh, well, you see, we've lost someone, and I wondered if you'd seen him.'

The wizard looked more interested at that.

'Lost someone? Someone else?'

'Yes, yes, we have,' explained Raven Boy. 'My rat. You haven't seen a lost rat around anywhere have you? His name's Rat.'

The wizard frowned and marched off.

'Ridiculous! Have I seen a rat? The castle's full of them!'

Elf Girl put her hand on Raven Boy's shoulder.

'Don't worry, we'll find him, I'm sure the wizard will help us. Maybe when he's less busy. Come on, we'd better keep up, you could get lost in this place and not be seen for days.'

They scooted after the wizard, who was still chattering, as much to himself as to them.

'Rats!' he said. 'The castle's full of them and he asks me if I've seen one! Ah, there you are again! Now then, I expect you're both needing a bit of a rest, aren't you?'

Raven Boy and Elf Girl nodded.

'Good, good,' said the wizard. 'We're nearly at your room, and then you can take it easy while I get everything ready. Excellent! This is all working out splendidly. You two are so helpful, you really are.'

Raven Boy and Elf Girl exchanged glances. They were both confused by at least half of what the wizard said, but they were too tired and hungry to care.

'Are you sure you haven't seen a very friendly rat?' Raven Boy asked again. 'Only we have to find him and then we have to cross the mountains, and the sea, and find the Goblin King.'

'The who?' asked the wizard.

'The Goblin King. He's evil and nasty and he's trying to destroy the whole world. He got an ogre to pull up the trees in our forest.'

'Goblin King,' said the wizard, looking thoughtful. 'Nope! Never heard of him. Come along now.'

They twisted this way and that through a few more tiny corridors, and then up a spiral staircase in a tower. Along to the end of another passageway, and down another spiral staircase. Finally, they stopped outside a simple door, which the wizard again opened with a key from inside his robe.

'Here we are! In you go, my dears!'

He stepped aside, smiling, and Raven Boy and Elf Girl entered the room.

'Er . . .' began Raven Boy.

'Yes, yes, what is it?'

'Is this our room?' he asked.

'Yes, yes. Wait here and I'll be back in a little while and then we can get on.'

Raven Boy looked around. There was almost nothing in the room, it was just bare

stone, with a single narrow window, and one old
wooden chair against the wall.

'But I thought we were going to have a
rest,' said Elf Girl. 'And have something to eat
too.'

'You can have a rest,' said the wizard. 'In fact, that would be good. Why don't you have a sleep on the floor? You'll look less tired if you do.'

'And food?' asked Raven Boy.

'Oh, definitely no food,' said the wizard, happily. 'No, no. It interferes with the process. Took me ages to work that out.'

'Process?' asked Raven Boy, who was beginning to have doubts about the castle, and the wizard and, in fact, everything to do with him.

'Yes, yes,' said the wizard. 'The process. You see, in the early days I'd let them have whatever they wanted, but the results were a little sloppy. But I've perfected the process now. I find it's much better on an empty stomach.'

'But we're starving!' cried Elf Girl.

'Yes, but that won't matter soon, will it?' laughed the wizard, in a jolly kind of way. 'Dear me, no. So you two just sit tight while I go and get ready, yes? Lovely, thank you so much.'

He was about to shut the door, when Raven Boy asked one more question.

'Excuse me? Mr Wizard. Sir Wizard, in fact. What, actually, is this process you keep talking about?'

'Oh!' cried the wizard, half in and half out of the room. 'Didn't I say? Silly me! The petrification process. For my collection. You two will make a lovely couple, and I've got a nice glass case that's just the right size too. Isn't that lucky? Now, now, I must be getting on. See you in a tick!'

With that, he whisked out of the room, shutting the door behind him. Raven Boy ran over to it, but was only in time to hear the key turn in the lock.

He tried the handle anyway, but the door didn't budge.

'Raven Boy?' asked Elf Girl, slowly.
'What does petrification mean?'

Raven Boy swallowed.

'It means being turned to stone,' he said,
in a very small voice.

'Yes, I thought it did,' Elf Girl said. 'I
just wanted to check.'

And with that, she fainted on the floor,
and Raven Boy could think of nothing better
than to do the same, and he joined her.

ELEVEN

Rat never used to go far from the riverbank until he met Raven Boy, but now he enjoys travelling curled up in Raven Boy's pocket.

'Why is it,' asked Elf Girl, when they'd woken up again, 'that everyone we meet wants to eat us or do something else to us that is going to shorten our lifespans?'

She was looking extremely cross, and Raven Boy felt that she thought it was his fault in some way.

'I don't know, Elf Girl,' he moaned.

'I guess there are a lot of mean people in the world. Or at least, there are in a place called Monster Mountains. That sign was right. Now we'll never find the Goblin King and save the forest!'

'Or find Rat,' added Elf Girl.

They both looked very glum indeed. Raven Boy wandered over to the window. Elf Girl picked herself up and plonked herself down on the single chair.

'Raven Boy?' she asked. 'Do you think it will hurt?'

'Being turned to stone?' said Raven Boy. 'I don't know, but it can't hurt more then being chewed by a yeti. Or trolls.'

'Oh yes,' said Elf Girl. 'The trolls! Well, that was one good thing. We won't be worrying about them any more.'

'Elf Girl, we won't be worrying about anything any more very soon. We'll be stone statues in his creepy collection.'

'I wonder what's in the collection,' said Elf Girl.

'Do you?' said Raven Boy.

'Didn't you see all those creatures on the way up here? They must have been his early attempts! When he was "perfecting his process!" Oh! I just want to get out of here, find Rat, and get out of these mountains.'

'So do I,' said Elf Girl, 'but how? The door's locked, and as for that window…'

What Elf Girl meant was that although the window wasn't locked, in fact, didn't even have any glass in it, there was a sheer drop straight down a cliff face that seemed to go on forever.

'You can't very well just nip down and get help, can you?'

'Can't I?' replied Raven Boy. 'Anyway, actually, I wasn't thinking of climbing down. I was thinking of climbing up. Look!'

Elf Girl went over to the window, stuck her head out and looked up. There was more of the sheer cliff face, but it didn't go so very far before it reached a stone balcony.

'You can't do it!' cried Elf Girl.

'Why not?' asked Raven Boy.

'It's too hard. The stonework is almost flat and if you slip… I don't want to wait around here by myself to be petrified while you turn yourself into strawberry jam on the rocks below!'

'Elf Girl! I'll be fine! Remember, climbing is what I do best.'

'But you climb trees, Raven Boy. Aren't rocks different?'

'No! Not at all,' said Raven Boy, then added, 'I think.'

'You mean, you've not done it before?'

'No, not exactly . . .'

'I won't allow it! That's final,' cried Elf Girl.

Raven Boy grabbed her elbows.

'Listen, if there was any other way, I'd do it, believe me. But there isn't. Any minute that crazy loon could come back and turn us into stone. I'll creep up the walls, get back in to the castle, and find something to open the door with. Or break it down. Okay? Wait here and don't be scared.'

Elf Girl nodded sadly, and with that Raven Boy set off.

She could hardly bear to watch him go. Through her fingers she saw him nimbly climb-

ing up the stone cliff face, finding tiny places to
put his toes and fingers.

Once he missed his footing and a shower of pebbles fell past Elf Girl. She shrieked, and watched as they fell down beneath her. She began to count, but had lost sight of the pebbles before she heard them hit anything.

'Oh,' she said, and looked up again, in time to see the back end of Raven Boy disappearing over the stonework of the balcony above.

'Hooray!' she cried. 'Raven Boy! You did it!'

Elf Girl turned away from the window, and looked around her. Suddenly she realised that she felt very scared.

She was all alone, in an almost empty room, with no way out, unless you were called Raven Boy, and at any moment, a mad wizard might return, ready to turn her into a garden ornament.

TWELVE

Jeremy the wizard might seem like a timid old man, but he's very powerful, and once turned an ogre into a squirrel.

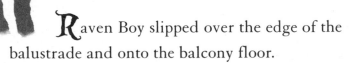

Raven Boy slipped over the edge of the balustrade and onto the balcony floor.

He looked down, the way he'd come, and felt a bit funny inside. He felt dizzy, too, and decided that it might be better to stop looking at the terrifying drop beneath him.

Not for the first time, he wondered what he was doing so far from home, from the forest and his animal friends. It was ages since he'd had a decent conversation with anything furry.

He tried to work out where he was.

The balcony was narrow, but had four tall glass doors that opened onto it, and a number of windows.

Raven Boy crept up to the first window and peeped in. There was no one there, and, feeling brave, he opened the glass door next to the window and let himself in.

He was in a long room, with rugs on the floor, and a large fireplace. There was a door at each end and from behind one he heard voices.

Feeling even braver, he crept over towards the door, and peeped through the keyhole.

There was the wizard, waving his arms as he talked. Raven Boy saw who he was talking to. Or rather, what.

On the table in the middle of the room was a glass ball and, inside it, he could see the face of another old man. For some reason, Raven Boy felt sure it was the face of another wizard, but whoever he was, he was chatting away to their wizard as if he was in the room for real.

'A crystal ball!' whispered Raven Boy.

'Ah! Jeremy,' said the wizard in the ball. 'How are you? All well? How's that nice collection of yours coming along?'

'Not too bad since you ask, Simon,' said the original wizard. 'Not too shabby at all. But listen, I've found another pair, and I'm about to add them to the gallery. Funny bird boy and an elf, I think. Anyway, they asked me something about the Goblin King . . .'

'The Goblin King?'

'Have you heard of him? They said he's trying to take over the world, or destroy it, or something? Have you ever heard of him?'

'Oh yes,' said Simon the wizard. 'He's big news in these parts. Thinking about upping and leaving, if you must know.'

'What what?' cried Jeremy. 'Don't say you're scared of him!'

'I'm not scared of him, old chap,' said Simon. 'What I am is terrified. You don't know what he can do! The magical powers he possesses! The evil! He makes me look like a naughty squirrel.'

'Isn't there anything you can do about it?'

Simon the wizard rolled his eyes.

'Yes, there is, but if you want to go on a wild-goose chase to find the Singing Sword and the Tears of the Moon, you go right ahead. They say that's the only magic strong enough to stop him, but I have a better idea.'

'What's that?'

'Run away and hide somewhere. Say, got any spare rooms in that castle of yours?

'Not one,' said Jeremy. 'Not a single one. Well, well, that's all very interesting. The Goblin King, eh . . . ?'

Outside the door, Raven Boy could only agree.

The Singing Sword? The Tears of the Moon?

He'd have to tell Elf Girl all about it.

He heard another voice inside the room, and put his eye back to the keyhole.

There was a strong and rather chunky-looking oaf standing there. That was the word that popped into Raven Boy's head, oaf, and once it was there, he couldn't do anything about it.

But it was a fair description. The man who stood in front of Jeremy the wizard was clearly a servant of some sort, and the look on his face could only be described as oafish.

'Simon, I'll have to go,' said Jeremy. 'Got these petrifications to do and now here's Clod come to bother me about something.'

'Very well! Let me know if you free up a spare room, eh?' said Simon, and with a small puff of cloud inside the crystal ball, he was gone.

Jeremy turned to Clod.

'Clod, can't you see I'm busy?'

Clod scratched his ear.

'Sorry, sir,' he said. 'Only I fink you ought to see something.'

'Oh what is it now?!' moaned the wizard. 'Honestly, Clod, this had better be good, I've got those two lovely dears all locked up and ready to go, and I'm itching to see how they turn out. I bet they are too.'

'But sir . . .'

'No, very well, I'm coming. I can see you've got your poor little brain all in a twist about something. Come along there, lead the way.'

Clod lurched towards the door at which
Raven Boy was eavesdropping, rather than the
one through which he must have come.

'EEP!' squeaked Raven Boy, and threw himself back onto the balcony, carefully closing the door behind him, just as Jeremy the wizard and Clod came into the room.

Raven Boy listened as their footsteps disappeared, then he counted to twenty, to make sure they'd really gone.

It was time to act!

The only problem was, he didn't know what to do. He had to find the way back to the room where Elf Girl was locked up, and he needed to find some way of opening the door. He wondered if he could burn it down, and how long that would take, even assuming he found something to burn it with.

He decided to take a quick look in the room where Jeremy had been speaking to Simon, and crept in cautiously to make sure no one else was there.

It was empty. He began to hunt for matches, or candles, or maybe even another magic wand he could use. The room was full of stuff; lots of strange objects, metal devices, peculiar-looking things in jars, books, maps, cupboards and shelves and drawers, and it was hard to know where to look first.

Suddenly, a voice behind him said, 'I say, one more thing, Jeremy.'

Raven Boy whirled round and saw Simon the wizard back in the crystal ball again, just as Simon spotted Raven Boy.

'Hey, you're not Jeremy,' he said. 'Who are you?'

'Er,' said Raven Boy, feeling slightly silly speaking to a ball, 'I'm, er, no one.'

'You must be someone. Hang on, I know who you are. You look like a bird, you're the bird boy he's got locked up! That's it!'

'No, really, I . . .'

Simon began to screech.

'Hey! Jeremy! Your bird boy's escaped! Hello! Are you there? Hello!'

'Stop it! Shh! Be quiet!' cried Raven Boy, but Simon was not about to stop.

'Hey! Je-remy! He-llo!'

'Stop it, I'm warning you!' declared Raven Boy. 'Be quiet, or . . .'

'Or you'll what?' sneered Simon. 'You can't do anything to me! Jeremy! Hey! Your bird-brain has escaped! Hello!'

'Right!' said Raven Boy, and he picked up the ball, and walked towards the window. 'I warned you!'

With his other hand he opened the window, and took a quick look outside. The same dizzying drop was underneath this one too.

'Wait, what are you doing?' asked

Simon. He sounded worried. 'You're not going to . . . Oh, no, no, you can't . . .'

'You asked for it!' cried Raven Boy, and he lobbed the ball out of the window.

'Noooooo!' came the voice of Simon, getting quieter very, very quickly, as he dropped like a stone.

'It was a stupid conversation anyway,' said Raven Boy, and began to hunt round the room for some matches.

Thirteen

Elf Girl is the most fashionable person she knows in the forest. She's still waiting for Raven Boy to notice.

Elf Girl was sitting on the chair in the room trying to make up games. She was doing that to pass the time, and as a way of trying not to think bad and scary thoughts, but she was finding it hard.

She'd already tried counting all the flag-stones on the floor, and then every stone in the walls, but it was too boring and she'd lost count.

Then she'd tried another game, which was to hold her breath for as long as she could. She was just wondering how to decide if she'd won the game or not when she passed out.

When she came round, she felt stupid.

'This really sucks,' she said, flopping down on the chair again, and then she felt very sorry for herself, locked in a room in a castle that belonged to a very naughty wizard.

She thought about Raven Boy, and about how they'd met, and how he'd saved them by getting help from a badger.

'I guess,' she said aloud, 'he's not bad for a boy. I wish he'd come back. I wish he'd come back soon.'

In fact, she was very, very scared indeed, and the only thing that stopped her feeling that way was when the sound of someone screaming fell past her window. She rushed to look out, and saw a glass ball dropping into the depths below.

'How odd,' she said, and sat down to think about it.

Raven Boy meanwhile had found a box of matches. At least, he thought they were matches. They were longer than usual, in fact, quite a bit longer than usual, and they were fatter too. There were only six of them and they were in a flat wooden box, with no writing or other markings on it. But they were made of wood and seemed to have a slightly wider bit of a different colour at the end, just like a normal match.

'Right,' he said. 'I can set fire to the door, and burn it down. It can't take that long, and then we can escape.'

With that, he clapped his hand over his mouth, he put the box in the inside pocket of his coat, and he set off to explore the castle.

He went back into the balcony room, the one with the glass doors.

'Elf Girl must be right below here,' he said. 'One floor down, maybe two. Nuts! I am going mad.'

Shutting his mouth tight, he crept as quietly as he could out of the room, hoping to find a flight of stairs that would take him down a floor or two to Elf Girl.

He didn't.

Instead he found himself in an octagonal hall with a further seven doors leading off from it. He opened a door at random and saw another corridor leading away.

He tried another door and found the same thing.

A third opened into a small room, with four more doors.

Raven Boy felt himself starting to panic, and tried to calm down. He went back into the octagonal room, and thought about what best to do.

Taking the door that was nearest to the outer wall of the castle, he opened it and set off.

He took a turn or two, went down a flight of steps and climbed up another, though there seemed to be no reason for either set of stairs.

He opened the next door he came to, and the next, and then began to run, hurtling through the castle in desperation, trying to find some way of getting his bearings, trying to find a way out.

He knew he ought to have kept a track of where he was going.

'At least,' he said, 'I knew I was right above Elf Girl in that first room! And now I'm going mad! Talking to myself! Crazy . . .'

He turned and tried to find his way back, back to the room with the balcony, planning to climb back the way he'd come, and set fire to the door from the inside.

'Why didn't I think of that before?' he cried.

'Because you're going mad,' he replied, to himself.

'Oh, I see. That makes sense.'

And then he stopped dead, because he realised he was lost. Totally and completely lost.

Fourteen

Jeremy and Simon met at wizard school, and have been friends ever since, though they only see each other in crystal balls these days.

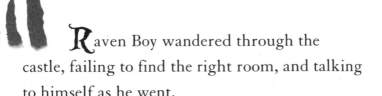

Raven Boy wandered through the castle, failing to find the right room, and talking to himself as he went.

'Ha! I really must be going mad. Talking to myself! If they ever find me again, they'll call me Raving Boy.'

Then he remembered that Elf Girl had already called him that once, and that worried him even more. It seemed she was right.

Eventually he found his way up a very
tall tower, at the top of which he came out onto
the parapet of a circular turret. From there,
he could see the whole castle, which seemed to
grow out of the rock. In places it was part of the
snow-covered mountains, in others, the stonework
of the castle was more obvious.

'I could be here for days and never find
Elf Girl again,' he sighed.

He looked up and out, back the way they'd

come, and then, walking around the turret, he looked at the way they'd intended to go.

The mountains stretched into the distance, and beyond them, he saw something else; a shiny, glittering strip of silver.

'The sea!' he cried, and felt excited and sad at the same time. He'd never seen the sea before, but he knew what it was because migrating birds had told him all about it.

'It's so far away, still, and I've lost Elf Girl and Rat now.'

He took a deep breath, and straightened his tatty black coat, pulling a feather from his hair.

'It's time to stop talking to myself, and stop going crazy. It's time to get on with getting us out of here. All of us!'

He stomped back into the tower. At least now he knew which side of the castle to head for, because he knew Elf Girl was somewhere on the side facing inland.

He turned this way and that, heading along more tiny passages, and then, just when he was sure he was getting close, he stumbled into a huge hall. It had windows all down one

side, high up, too high to see out of. There was
a wooden table in the centre of the room, and
a vast sparkling chandelier hanging from the
centre of the ceiling.

Raven Boy saw none of this, however.
What caught his eye were the glass cases lining
the room and, inside the cases, the animals, and
people. And several large scary-looking monsters,
quite like the things he'd seen on the
mountain: Jeremy's early attempts
at petrification.

He guessed he had found
Jeremy the wizard's collection.

Cautiously, timidly,
Raven Boy crept into the room
and went up to the nearest case.

Inside was a short man,
smaller even than Raven Boy.
The man held a crook, and
Raven Boy guessed he was a
shepherd. He seemed so lifelike, as
if he might move at any moment,
but he was grey from head to
foot, made of stone.

In the next case were two tall men, dressed in warm clothes. They had big boots with spikes on them, and long ropes wrapped in a coil slung over their shoulders. Now Raven Boy noticed that there were small brass labels pinned to the bottom of each case.

'Mountaineers,' Raven Boy read on this one.

He moved on. Next there was a woodcutter. In the next case he found a goat, like the one that had biffed them earlier, but smaller. There were more animals, a few sheep and then some birds; some crows and a few small kestrels, which brought a tear to Raven Boy's eye.

And in the final case, a display of rats. There was one massive rat, King Rat, turned to stone, and all the rest were stone too.

It was spooky, and Raven Boy was scared, and a bit sad, because his own little Rat was still missing.

Stone. Everyone turned to stone!

So this was what the wizard wanted to do to him and Elf Girl!

As if he needed further proof, he came to an empty case at the far end of the room. Raven Boy bent over to read the brass label.

'Girl Elf and Bird Boy,' it said.

'At least get my name right!' said Raven Boy crossly then, realising someone might hear him, he listened for any sound. He heard nothing, but, looking back at the room of stone statues, he knew there was no time to waste.

As soon as Jeremy had finished with whatever it was that Clod wanted to show him, he'd be coming back to do what he'd threatened; turn Raven Boy and Elf Girl into the latest exhibits in his collection of petrified people.

'EeP!' peeped Raven Boy, and he sped away into the castle, even more desperate than before.

Fifteen

The castle is home to thousands of rats, all ruled by King Rat, that is until Jeremy turned him into stone for campering up and down and making scratching noises on the floorboards, which kept Jeremy awake all night.

Meanwhile, back in the locked room with the single chair, Elf Girl couldn't decide whether she was more bored than frightened, or more frightened than bored.

'I wonder,' she said, 'if you can actually be bored and frightened at the same time? That's something to think about.'

And she was glad of that, because it gave her something to do for at least three minutes, until she realised she was bored of thinking about it.

'Bother!' she said aloud. 'And nuts.'

She stomped over to the window, where she had already spent a lot of time, gazing at the snowy mountains, and occasionally peering up to see if Raven Boy was coming back.

She really did feel as if she was going bonkers, and was about to scream, when there was the rattle of a key in the lock, and the door swung open.

Then she did scream, because into the room walked three men. There was a big one, a middle-sized one and a little one, and Elf Girl recognised them as the three trolls from the Fright Forest, only, being daytime, they were in their human form.

'What's all that fuss?' said Jeremy, as he followed them in. 'Now then, I'm sure there's no need for all that noise, is there?'

Elf Girl felt differently.

'I think there is,' she declared. 'These three men aren't men at all. They're trolls! And they're trying to eat us. You can't bring them in here.'

Jeremy looked puzzled for a minute, and then turned to the trio.

'Is this true?' he asked. 'Are you trolls? Actually?'

The little one looked rather proud.

'As it 'appens, yeah. We are trolls.'

'But you don't look like trolls,' said Jeremy.

'Oh no, well, ye see, that's because we only become trolls at night. See?'

'Really?' cried Jeremy. 'How fascinating! Well, it is my lucky day, isn't it? How nice to have bumped into you gentleman wandering through my castle like that.'

'When do we get to eat sumfin' anyway?' asked the big man.

'Stupid troll!' cried Elf Girl. 'You won't get to eat anything. He's going to turn you into stone, just like he wants to turn Raven Boy and me into stone too!'

The three looked at each other for a long time, and then burst out laughing.

'No!' cried Elf Girl. 'It's true.'

'Can we eat the girl now?' asked the middle-sized one, when he'd stopped laughing.

'Oh, no,' said Jeremy. 'Absolutely not. You see, it interferes with the process.'

'The process?' asked the little one.

'Oh, yes, the petrification process.'

'Peter-fer-whatsit?' said the big one.

'I told you!' yelled Elf Girl. 'He's going to turn you into stone, and put you in a glass case!'

The trolls began laughing again, and Jeremy laughed too.

'Yes, it is fun, isn't it? Listen, I'd love to stay and chat some more, but I have to get everything ready and I'm going to need to see if I have a case big enough for you three or if you'll have to go in one each.'

The men-trolls stopped laughing and began to understand.

'Ere . . .' the big one said, and began to walk towards Jeremy, looking tough and mean and cross all at once.

'Ah, yes, since we can't have any little problems like that, I suppose . . .'

With that, Jeremy pulled his wand out of his pocket and waved it at the trolls. Then he waved it at Elf Girl who, like the trolls, suddenly

found herself sitting against the wall of the
room, with her hands bound in iron shackles,
attached to the wall.

'There,' said Jeremy. 'That's better, isn't
it? Now no one can do anything silly like try and
escape. You four just get along now for a while,

and I'll go and get things ready downstairs, okay? Good. How lovely. Of course, we'll have to wait until the evening now; I'd much rather have three trolls in my collection than three rather ugly men . . .'

'Oi!' cried the middle-sized one.

Elf Girl laughed.

'You don't frighten me!' she called to the wizard, as he left the room.

'How nice,' said Jeremy.

'No!' cried Elf Girl. 'And furthermore,' she added, 'Raven Boy has escaped. By now he'll be miles from here, getting lots of help. From animals, and things . . . Really big, angry ones, and they'll come here and flatten your stinky castle and turn you into stone yourself. Somehow.'

'Raven Boy?' asked Jeremy. 'Raven Boy? Do you mean the little chap who was with you before?'

Elf Girl nodded.

'Oh, that's a shame, I've got his name wrong on the label . . . Anyway, here he is now. I'll see you in a bit.'

Jeremy stepped aside, and Raven Boy floated into the room, at the end of Clod's arm.

'He seems to have got lost in the castle, silly chap! Luckily, Clod found him. We can't have that happen again, can we?'

Jeremy waved his wand, and Raven Boy was sitting next to Elf Girl, chained to the wall, just like her.

'Oh, Raven Boy,' said Elf Girl. 'You've made me look a bit stupid. But I'm glad to see you anyway.'

'I'm sorry,' said Raven Boy sadly. 'I did my best, but this place is so huge, I kept on getting lost.'

'Oi!' said the little troll. 'Wizard!'

'His name's Jeremy,' Raven Boy pointed out.

'Oi, Jeremy!' said the little one again. 'You can't just leave us here! Come back here and I'll bite your arms off!'

'Really?' said Jeremy, smiling as broadly as ever. 'That would be rather silly of me, then, wouldn't it? I'll let the five of you have a nice little chat, and we'll see you at sunset.

Marvellous! Come along, Clod, there's lots to do, lots to do.'

The key rattled in the lock once more, and the sound of their footsteps faded away.

Raven Boy and Elf Girl looked at each other, then at the three trolls.

Then back at each other.

'EEP!' cheeped Raven Boy.

Sixteen

**When a troll changes into a human
at daybreak, it hurts. But not as
much as when they change back into
a troll at sunset. Not a pretty sight,
even to other trolls.**

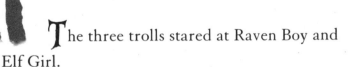

The three trolls stared at Raven Boy and
Elf Girl.

'Er, hello,' said Raven Boy.

'We are going to eat you so much,' said
the middle-sized one, 'when we get out of here,
see?'

Elf Girl's ears went pink.

'Really! Why? What's wrong with you
three, anyway? Ever since we met you you've

been trying to eat us!'

'Yeah,' said the little one, 'that's what we do, see?'

'No, I do not see,' said Elf Girl. 'And even if I did, it's one thing to have eaten us in the forest, but you've been following us for days! Isn't that a bit weird?'

'Oh, no,' said the little one, explaining. 'You see, we're big and scary trolls, right?'

He looked at his companions.

'Right,' they agreed.

'And if word got around that we let two puny, scrawny, feeble-weeble little fings like you get away . . . People wouldn't think we were so scary and big any more, would they?'

'Right,' said the other two.

'And so you see, that's bad for a troll. A lot of what we do is based around the scary stuff. It makes life easier, doesn't it, boys?'

The other two nodded their heads energetically.

'Yeah, you see, sometimes people just drop down dead when we meet them. And that saves a whole lot of trouble. Whereas you two,

you two . . .' and here
the little one began to
get cross, '. . . you two
have caused us no end
of bother. And we don't
like bother. What we like
is nice little children who
get eaten when they're
supposed to. See?'

He was so cross
that he tugged at his
chains and made chomping noises with his teeth
in their direction.

'Ha, ha!' said Raven Boy, trying to
pretend that it was all a joke. He failed. 'You
know,' he went on, 'I'm sure this is all some big
misunderstanding.'

'Really?' sneered the middle-sized troll.

'Really?' squeaked Elf Girl.

'Yes,' said Raven Boy, 'really. You see,
I'm sure no one really wants to eat anyone here.'

The big troll opened his mouth to speak
and Raven Boy went on hurriedly before anyone
could interrupt him.

'No, no, not really. Well, I think it's just because we haven't been properly introduced.'

'Intra-juiced?' asked the big one.

'Yes,' said Raven Boy.

'Really?' said Elf Girl.

'Yes, really. Introduced. You see, I can speak to the animals . . . '

'Raven Boy,' whispered Elf Girl, 'is this helping?'

'And when you can speak to the animals, it rather changes the way you feel about eating them, see?'

'No,' said the little one. 'I don't see.'

'Well, let's try anyway,' said Raven Boy. 'I'm Raven Boy and this is Elf Girl. We're pleased to meet you. How do you do?'

Raven Boy nudged Elf Girl.

'Ow. What? Oh,' she said. She looked at the three trolls. 'I'm pleased to meet you too. How do you do?'

'How do we do what?' asked the big one.

'See?' said Elf Girl to Raven Boy. 'They're too stupid to even begin to understand how to be nice.'

'Oi, watch it,' said the middle one. 'Who are you calling stupid?'

He rattled his chains.

'Just you wait till sunset,' he growled. 'Then we turns into trolls and I'll pull this thing out of the wall in no time.'

'And supposing you can't?' said Raven Boy.

'"Course I can,' said the middle-sized one.

'Are you sure? These are magic chains. Supposing you can't break them, even as a troll? And then, at sunset, Jeremy the evil wizard is coming back to turn us into stone. All of us. Even you.'

The trolls looked thoughtful.

'So don't you think, maybe, it might be best to try and work together and get us out of here, and stop all this talk about eating people?'

The trolls looked even more thoughtful, which seemed to be quite difficult for them.

'Now,' said Raven Boy, 'I'm Raven Boy and this is Elf Girl. What are your names? Do you, er, have names?'

'Of course we does!' snapped the little one.

'Jolly good!' cried Raven Boy. 'So? What are your names?'

The trolls looked at each other, and began whispering among themselves. It seemed as if they were having an argument.

Elf Girl took the chance to whisper to Raven Boy.

'Raven Boy? What are you doing? Making friends with them?'

'I just think,' he said, 'that if we get to know them, and they get to know us, that they won't want to eat us so much. Or not at all, hopefully. Like I said, it's very hard to eat a wood pigeon when you were talking to his uncle the day before. If they know our names and we have a little chat . . .'

'We'll do you a deal,' said the little one.

'Er, okay, what is it?' asked Raven Boy.

'We'll tell you our names, and we'll work together to get us out of here, so that none of us get petraficated, right?'

'Right.'

'On one condition,' the troll went on. 'Which is, as soon as we're out of here, you have to let us try and eat you again.'

Elf Girl looked at Raven Boy.

'Crazy,' she mouthed. 'Cray-zee.'

'It's a deal,' said Raven Boy, quickly.

'What?' cried Elf Girl.

'What have we got to lose?' Raven Boy said, shrugging and clanging his chains, reminding Elf Girl of their sticky situation.

'Fair enough,' she said, shrugging.

'Right,' said Raven Boy, 'it's a deal. So, come on then, what are you called?'

'I'm called Bert,' said the little one. 'Pleased to meet ya. Right?'

Raven Boy nodded, smiling.

'And this,' said Bert, nodding at the

middle-sized one, 'is Bob. Say hello, Bob.'

''Ello,' said Bob.

'And this,' Bert went on, nodding at the big troll, 'is Cedric.'

'Cedric!' cried Raven Boy, and he and Elf Girl burst out laughing.

Cedric was hopping mad.

'I told ya they'd larf at me. I told ya,' he said, angrily to Bert. 'Why d'ya 'ave to tell 'em, eh? Why?'

Raven Boy and Elf Girl did their best to stop laughing.

'Sorry, Cedric,' Raven Boy said, trying not to snigger. 'We're sorry, aren't we, Elf Girl? After all, we have pretty silly names too, don't we, Elf Girl? Our real names, I mean. Hers is…'

Elf Girl reached out her foot and kicked Raven Boy's ankle so hard he yelled.

'Don't you dare!' she said, and Raven Boy saw from the pinkness of her ears that it would be best not to reveal Elf Girl's real name. Not just then.

'Good,' said Raven Boy. 'Well, now that we've all been properly introduced, let's come up with a plan.'

SEVENTEEN

Raven Boy's real name begins
with an R, but he thinks it's so
embarrassing he'll never
admit it to anyone.

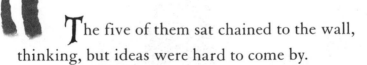

The five of them sat chained to the wall,
thinking, but ideas were hard to come by.

'I've got a box of matches,' said Raven
Boy brightly, after a while.

'That's good to know,' said Elf Girl.

'Is she being sar-car-stic?' Bob asked Bert.

'Seriously big matches, I mean,' Raven
Boy went on, ignoring her. 'We could burn the

door down!'

'And even if we could get the matches from your coat and light them with our toes, we'd still be chained to the wall, wouldn't we, genius.'

Raven Boy was silent, because Elf Girl had a good point. Trust her.

'I wonder,' said Bert, 'how long the sun is going to stay up today.'

'Not much longer,' said Elf Girl, looking out of the window. 'It's getting dark.'

'Right then,' said Bert.

'Right then, what?' asked Raven Boy.

'Right then, we'll find out how strong these magic chains are, won't we? When the sun goes down, and we turn back into trolls.'

The other two sniggered.

'Are you going to turn into trolls, right in front of us?' asked Elf Girl.

'We don't have much choice, do we?' said Bob.

'Is it messy? Does it smell?' asked Elf Girl.

'Shh, Elf Girl,' said Raven Boy. 'That's not very polite.'

'Well, they do whiff a bit, even as men,' said Elf Girl. She wrinkled her nose.

'I know,' whispered Raven Boy, 'but I do think it might not be a good idea to upset them. Just in case.'

'Yes, you're right,' said Elf Girl. 'It's just that I can't stand not knowing what's going to happen.'

'What's going to happen,' said Bert, 'is that the sun is about to set, and when it does, ping! We'll have these chains off in two shakes. Right, boys?'

'Right!' said the other two.

It was indeed true. The sun was setting, and the three trolls craned their necks towards the window, waiting for the last rays to disappear.

The room got a little darker, and then Cedric began to chuckle.

''Ere we go again,' he said.

The sun set, and almost as soon as it had, the three men started to turn into Bert, Bob and Cedric, the fearsome trolls.

Raven Boy and Elf Girl watched with open mouths as the change took place. There was a lot of squirming and wriggling, like they had ants in their pants, or something worse. They were making all sorts of funny faces too.

'Ooh,' said Elf Girl. 'Look!'

'Shh,' said Raven Boy, 'I am looking!'

All in all it took five minutes for the men to become their true and horrible selves, and Raven Boy and Elf Girl watched in amazement as the trolls sprouted hair, their ears got bigger and their faces became even more ugly. Green warts grew and yellow fingernails got longer and dirtier, and finally, with a funny popping sound, it was all over.

'Ow,' said Cedric, 'That 'urts.'

'Aw, Cedric,' said Bert. 'Do yer 'ave to say that every time?'

'But it does,' said Cedric, sulkily.

'Right, then, never mind that. Let's get these chains off, yeah?'

Cedric and Bob nodded.

'Only,' said Bert, 'let's do it together, on three.'

'Why?' asked Cedric.

''Cos it'll look more impressive that way,' said Bert.

'Oh yeah. Good idea,' said Bob.

'Right, here we go then,' cried Bert.

'One...'

'Er, excuse me,' said Raven Boy. 'Only, you are going to keep your promise, aren't you?'

'Two . . .' said Bert.

'And get us out of here and not eat us yet?' added Elf Girl.

'Hurr, hurr, hurr,' said Cedric, with a most evil chuckle.

'Three!' cried Bert. 'Now!'

All three trolls tugged at their chains at once, and precisely nothing happened.

They tugged again.

Nothing: the chains did not move even the tiniest bit.

'Oh, blast it,' said Bob, very grumpily.

They all tried once more, and then collapsed panting and heaving and out of breath.

'Well,' said Raven Boy. 'That's that.'

'We're as good as petrified already,' wailed Elf Girl.

'Squeak!' said Rat, and Raven Boy and Elf Girl nearly jumped out of their skins in delight.

They turned their heads to see Rat, as

bold as you please, sticking his head in under
the door of the cell.

He squeaked again, twice, quite urgently.
'What's he saying?' asked Elf Girl.
Raven Boy nodded at Rat.
'He's been looking for us for ages. He
followed our tracks in the snow, and saw the
yeti footprints. He sniffed about and found one
of my feathers, and then he smelt the castle.
When he got here, he spoke to the castle rats,
and they told him where we were. Only he says
he can hear footsteps coming. Right now!'

'Oh, no!' cried Elf Girl. 'That's it! We're doomed!'

'Run, Rat!' cried Raven Boy. 'Run, and get help. You're our only hope now! Run as fast as you can!'

Rat gave two high-pitched squeaks, and ducked back out under the door.

Moments later, came the sound of the key in the lock again, and the door swung open.

There was Jeremy, with Clod behind him.

'Is everyone ready?' Jeremy asked, smiling in a friendly way. 'Good, good! Been having a nice chat? That's super. Passes the time, doesn't it?'

Everyone stared at him as if he was crazy, which, to be honest, he probably was.

'Right, up you all get then. Let's go and get you all nicely petrified! I can hardly wait, and I bet you're excited too. You're all going to look so lovely. Wait till you see what I've got ready for you. A nice little surprise, and everyone likes surprises, don't they?'

Raven Boy and Elf Girl looked at each other.

'No,' said Raven Boy. 'Actually, I'm not that keen on surprises. Not right now.'

But Jeremy was not listening, and with a wave of his wand, all five were on their feet, and though their chains were off the walls, they were still chained together, unable to get away.

'That,' said Jeremy to Raven Boy, 'is not very nice of you, is it? When I've gone to such trouble. Do come along and see. You never know, you might change your mind!'

With that, they left, and Elf Girl noticed that even the trolls' knees were shaking, they were so scared.

EIGHTEEN

If you live in treetops, it's hard to go shopping, but Raven Boy's been lucky and got everything he wears from things people have thrown away.

The five trooped along in a sad line, with Clod leading the way and Jeremy at the back.

They tramped along and very soon came to the room that Raven Boy had seen before, with the glass cases and, inside them, the stone statues.

'Good!' cried Jeremy, who was quite over-excited by now, because the end of his wand was quivering. 'Here we are! Look!'

He pointed to the end of the row, and Raven Boy saw that the empty glass case had disappeared and been replaced by a new, larger one.

'Have a look!' said Jeremy, and they stomped dismally over to the case.

'What's it say?' asked Cedric.

Elf Girl read the label.

'Raven Boy and Elf Girl are caught by three ugly trolls.'

'Oi!' cried Cedric.

'At least he got my name right this time,' said Raven Boy.

'Well, 'e didn't use our names, at all!' cried Bert, huffily. 'That's not fair!'

'Good, lovely,' said Jeremy. 'Now, it's very simple, all I need you to do is stand in a nice pose. If you two could act terrified, and you three wave your arms in the air, as if you're about to catch them and eat them. That would be lovely.'

'And why are we going to do that, exactly?' asked Elf Girl.

'Obviously,' said Jeremy, 'my scene isn't going to work if you don't, is it?'

'There's just no talking to you, is there?' said Raven Boy.

'You can talk to me as much as you like,' said Jeremy, beaming. 'Now come along, I want to call my friend Simon and show him my new exhibit.'

'Good luck with that,' muttered Raven Boy.

Fortunately Jeremy either didn't hear him, or chose to ignore him.

'Come along,' Jeremy said, sounding impatient now. 'We don't have all night. Come on. You two need to look terrified…'

'That shouldn't be hard,' said Elf Girl.

Raven Boy looked very miserable, but he couldn't see what else to do. The wizard's magic was too strong to fight, and as long as he kept waving the wand around, there was no way of stopping him. One flick and they'd all be stone, or whatever else he chose to turn them into, presumably.

Slowly, Raven Boy and Elf Girl climbed in through the back of the glass case.

'Oh, look,' said Elf Girl. 'There's my bow!'

She pointed to a separate case, a little way away, in which she could see her magic bow.

'Oh that's yours, is it?' said Jeremy. 'I wondered about that. The yeti was using it as a tooth-pick. I'll turn that to stone too and add it to your display.'

Elf Girl longed for her bow, but there was no way to get it. She climbed into the glass case.

'Good,' said Jeremy, as Raven Boy and Elf Girl got into position. 'Now, you three. In you go.'

The three trolls were about to lumber in, when Raven Boy cried out.

'Yay!' he said, and began waving his arms.

'No!' said Jeremy, 'that's not right. What are you doing? Stop it!'

But Elf Girl was doing it too now, because she'd seen what Raven Boy had seen.

'Yay!'

The three trolls had seen it too, and began to lollop and dance in the strangest way. All five were looking behind Jeremy and Clod, who turned round to see what all the fuss was about.

The fuss turned out to be rats. Thousands of them, all scampering towards the wizard at high speed. Every one of them was snow white, and they had pink eyes and chubby little tails. They poured out of every hole and nook and cranny in the walls, and had formed a huge mass, charging towards one very surprised-looking wizard.

'Oh no you don't,' he cried, and pointed his wand, and began shooting little bolts of lightning at the rats, but they were too small and too fast, and dodged his shots as easily as if it were a game.

There, at the head of the horde, was Rat himself.

In a second, they were on Jeremy, and began chewing and nibbling him so hard that he toppled over, and began to roll around on the floor. He waved his wand wildly, but uselessly, as he was completely helpless.

'No! Get off!' he cried. 'That tickles, stop it! Get off!'

Calmly, Elf Girl sauntered over to him and plucked the wand from his hand.

'There!' she said. 'I'll take that, thanks very much.'

Raven Boy called to Rat.

'That's enough! You can stop now!'

It took Rat and the others a long time to understand that they'd done enough, but they stopped in the end.

They clambered off Jeremy, but formed a ratty circle around him, in case he tried anything.

Jeremy got to his feet. His good humour had finally disappeared.

'You horrible, nasty . . .'

'Now, now,' said Raven Boy. 'I'm sure there's no need for that sort of talk.'

'Give me my wand back, you mean little witch,' he growled, trying to move towards Elf Girl. 'You don't know how to use it anyway.'

Elf Girl flicked the wand in Jeremy's direction and shot a bolt of lightning between his feet.

'Don't I? It seems simple enough.'

'Elf Girl!' cried Raven Boy. 'How did you do that?'

Elf Girl shook her head.

'I'm not sure. It sort of feels right,' she said.

'Do you think you could do something else with it?'

'What did you have in mind?'

Raven Boy pointed at all the cases, and all the people and animals inside them.

'Do you think you can bring them back to life again? All except the monsters maybe.'

NINETEEN

Although he's called Raven Boy, he can't actually fly, though he'd really like to learn one day soon.

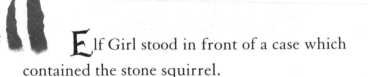

Elf Girl stood in front of a case which contained the stone squirrel.

She was very nervous, because the last thing she wanted to do was make things worse, and blow it to bits with a lightning bolt.

Finally, she shut her eyes, and waved the wand.

There was a puff of smoke, and then,

jumping up and down in the case, a very happy-looking squirrel indeed.

Raven Boy laughed and opened the case. The squirrel jumped straight out and onto his head, and he laughed again.

'Quick! Do everyone else,' he cried. 'Do the rats!'

'No!' wailed Jeremy. 'Stop that! You have no right!'

'Be quiet,' Elf Girl said, 'or we'll set the rats on you again.'

Jeremy suddenly looked worried, and shut his mouth, while Elf Girl and Raven Boy ran round from case to case, bringing everyone back to life. Finally, Elf Girl waved her wand at King Rat, and he sprang to life, squeaking like crazy and saying hello to all his friends.

Very soon, there was laughter and talking and people explaining what had happened to them.

'He caught me in the forest,' said the woodcutter.

'And told us to stand still,' said the mountaineers.

Then, the chatting died down, and people began to get angry. They surrounded the wizard, waving their fists at him and shouting.

Finally, Raven Boy managed to get everyone to calm down.

'Listen,' he said to Jeremy. 'You've been very bad and done some awful things. These poor people have been stuck here for ages, and might have stayed here forever. And we might have joined them if Rat hadn't saved the day! So what do you have to say for yourself?'

Jeremy scowled at Raven Boy.

'Nothing!'

'Well, at the very least, you have to promise to give up doing nasty things, and turning people and animals into stone. Right?'

'Hah,' cried Jeremy. 'Wrong. I shall make no such promise.'

'Really?' demanded Raven Boy. 'This is your last chance.'

'Never!'

Raven Boy turned to Elf Girl.

'Right, then,' he said, and Elf Girl shut her eyes again and waved the wand at Jeremy.

A second later, a cloud of smoke cleared around Jeremy, and there he was, standing as still as a statue, made of stone.

Everyone cheered, and then two strong men lifted him into place inside a case, and shut the door.

Everyone cheered again.

'Right!' cried Elf Girl, 'time to get out of here. Clod, look after your wizard, won't you?'

Everyone laughed, and Elf Girl was laughing just as much, when suddenly Bert stepped up behind her, and snatched the wand from her hand.

'I'll have that,' he said, 'thank you very much. Very interesting little thing, that is . . .'

'Now, wait a minute,' Raven Boy shouted, stepping forward. 'You promised to help us!'

'Only till we were free,' said Bert. 'So, too bad!'

'You're a nasty stinky troll!'

'Now then,' said Bert, chuckling. 'I'm sure there's no need for talk of that sort.'

He began to wave the wand around.

'I wonder how this works . . .' he said.

'You mean, rotten, smelly . . .' began Elf Girl, but she stopped, as Bert pointed the wand right at her and gave it a little flick.

Elf Girl shrieked, and there was a blinding flash, and a huge ball of smoke, all from where Bert stood.

When the smoke disappeared, there he was, with burnt eyebrows, singed clothes and soot on his face. He looked very cross indeed. The wand was nowhere to be seen.

The three trolls looked at Raven Boy and Elf Girl, and at everyone else, and began to walk forward menacingly. Even the rats looked scared, and they, and everyone else, began to back away.

Then Bert shouted, 'Get 'em!'

They charged and everyone ran as fast as they could, and Elf Girl grabbed her bow as she ran past its case.

'Shall I try . . . ?' she shouted to Raven Boy, but he just shouted, 'No time! Run!'

And he was right, because the trolls were nearly upon them.

People scattered this way and that, heading anywhere, but the trolls only seemed to want to get revenge on Raven Boy, Elf Girl and Rat, who were soon pounding down corridor after corridor with the trolls hot on their tail.

'Quick!' wailed Raven Boy. 'They're fast!'

'I know!' yelled Elf Girl.

They burst into another room and slid to a stop. There was nowhere to run. A dead end. The room had a few suits of armour and a furry rug, and a glass door that led on to another balcony. And that was about it. Nothing to help them.

Bert, Bob and Cedric burst into the room, and slid to a halt too.

'Haw, haw!' chuckled Cedric. 'We got 'em!'

'Raven Boy!' cried Elf Girl. 'What do we do now?'

Raven Boy looked around frantically.

'Try your bow!'

Elf Girl did, but for some reason, all she managed to do was produce a flurry of snow.

'Ooh, stop it,' said Bert. 'I'll catch a cold.'

'I'm sorry, Raven Boy,' said Elf Girl. 'I just can't get the hang of this thing!'

But the snow had given Raven Boy an idea. He grabbed the shield from one of the suits of armour, and handed it to Elf Girl. Then, taking another for himself, they ran on to the balcony.

Raven Boy looked over the edge.

'Right,' he said.

'Right what?' asked Elf Girl, but then she understood. 'No! Oh, no! No, you can't be serious!'

'I certainly am,' cried Raven Boy.

The trolls were hurtling towards them.

'Jump!' cried Raven Boy.

And they did.

TWENTY

Once, Raven Boy and Elf Girl managed to go a whole day without squabbling. But only once.

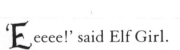

'Eeeee!' said Elf Girl.

'Eeeee!' cried Raven Boy, and this time, it was not from fear, but from fun.

'Squeak!' squeaked Rat, sitting on Raven Boy's head, where he belonged.

They'd dropped on to the snowy banks of the mountainside, and were riding the shields they'd stolen from the suits of armour across the snow, just as if they were on toboggans.

They were picking up speed all the time, and though it was a dark night, they didn't feel scared. They were so pleased to have escaped the trolls, the castle and the mean wizard Jeremy.

Down and down they sped, faster and faster, until finally Elf Girl called to Raven Boy.

'How do we stop?'

'I didn't think of that!' Raven Boy cried out.

'Oh! Raven Boy!' wailed Elf Girl. 'What'll we do when we hit the bottom?'

'Stop, I suppose,' Raven Boy shouted back.

The snow was flying in their faces, and trees whipped by on either side, and suddenly it didn't seem so much fun any more.

'No brakes!' wailed Raven Boy.

On and on they slid, and then they passed the edge of the snow.

'We must be nearly at the bottom,' shouted Raven Boy.

But still they kept sliding, on grass now, until finally, the hill levelled out and they crashed into a large haystack.

'Well,' said Raven Boy. 'That was fun.'

'I vote we don't do it again,' said Elf Girl. 'Soon, anyway.'

'Look,' said Raven Boy. 'There's a hut. We can spend the night there, and then see where we are in the morning, when it's light.'

'Good idea,' agreed Elf Girl and, dragging their shields with them, they hid in the hut.

In the morning, they woke early.

'I'm so hungry,' said Elf Girl.

'We've had nothing to eat for ages,' said Raven Boy. 'At least we're back in a forest now. We can find something to eat, I'm sure. Let's get going.'

'Which way?' asked Elf Girl.

'Downhill, of course,' said Raven Boy. 'I forgot to tell you, I saw the sea from the top of the castle. And the sea's always downhill, isn't it?'

'I've never seen the sea,' said Elf Girl.

'Nor me, not properly. What fun!'

They set off, and soon found some nuts and tasty berries to eat and were feeling much happier altogether when, suddenly, Raven Boy stopped.

'Wait!' he said.

'What is it?' asked Elf Girl.

'I heard something. Someone's following us.'

'Are you sure?' asked Elf Girl.

'Yes! Quick! Up this tree.'

They climbed as fast as they could, and not a moment too soon, because just as they got out of sight, Bert, Bob and Cedric passed by, right underneath them.

They stopped, and sniffed.

'What's that smell?' said Bert, looking up. 'Good morning! Thought you'd got away from us, didn't you?'

'Oh, no,' moaned Elf Girl and Raven Boy.

Rat squeaked and went to hide in Raven Boy's pocket.

'So,' said Bert. 'What's it going to be? Do yer want to come down now and save us all a lot of waitin'?'

'I hate waitin',' said Cedric. 'It's really borin'.'

'Yes, I know,' said Bert. 'Or,' he added to Raven Boy and Elf Girl, 'do you want to wait until we turn into trolls again, by which time we'll be really angry?'

'Hmm,' said Raven Boy. 'That is quite a choice . . .'

'Oh, what are we going to do?' Elf Girl

said, her eyes gaping.

'You could try your bow again,' suggested Raven Boy.

Elf Girl looked sad.

'I will,' she said, 'but I seem to have lost the trick of using it again. I thought I had it all sorted out.'

She slung the bow around and tried to fire at the trolls, who were already laughing at her.

'What's it gonna be this time?' sniggered Bob. 'Bird seed?!'

Absolutely nothing happened at all.

'Oh Raven Boy,' moaned Elf Girl. 'I don't get it. And yet I used the magician's wand just fine.'

'I don't understand either,' said Raven Boy, looking thoughtful. Then he fished in his pocket, and pulled out the box he'd found in the wizard's room.

'You know,' he said, 'I've been thinking. I thought I'd found a box of matches, but you know, the more and more I think about it . . .'

He took out one of the matches and handed it to Elf Girl.

'What does that look like to you?' he

asked her.

Elf Girl looked at it, hard.

'This sounds silly,' she said. 'Only . . .'

'Only what?' asked Raven Boy. 'What do
you think it is?'

'Well, it looks just like the wizard's
wand, only smaller.'

'That's exactly what I was thinking . . .'
he said, smirking. 'Do you want to have a try,
with those three?'

Elf Girl nodded.

She pointed the tiny
wand down at the trolls, and
waved it, with a quick flick.

There was a puff of smoke,
and there was Bert, with his trousers
on fire. He shrieked, and ran off into
the woods.

'It worked!'
cried Elf Girl.
'Only the wand
disappeared!'

'Well! A
one-use wand,' said

Raven Boy. 'Fancy that!
Here, there are five left,
you can use two more on
Bob and Cedric.'

Elf Girl did, and
in no time, the other two
were hurrying away after
Bert, trying to find some
water to put out the fire on
their bottoms.

Raven Boy and Elf
Girl climbed down from the tree,
and Raven Boy put the three
tiny wands back in his pocket.

'Those could come in very handy,' he said.
'Well done, Elf Girl.'

Elf Girl smiled, but she still seemed
unhappy.

'I just wish I knew how to make my bow
work every time.'

'You will,' said Raven Boy. 'I'm sure.
One day.'

They walked on and on through the forest,
and as they went, Raven Boy told Elf Girl what

he'd heard Jeremy saying to Simon, about the Goblin King, and what Simon had told him, about the Singing Sword and the Tears of the Moon.

'That's great,' said Elf Girl. 'Only what are they?'

'I don't know,' said Raven Boy.

'And where are they?'

'I don't know that either, but at least we know there might be a way to fight the Goblin King.'

Elf Girl nodded.

She smiled.

'And there's some more good news,' she said, and pointed.

Then they both began to run, because they'd seen something more magical than a wizard's wand.

There was the sea, just beyond the edge of the trees, and they ran on to the beach, laughing and kicking sand at each other.

'We made it!' laughed Elf Girl.

'Yes!' said Raven Boy. 'And now it's time to cross the sea, find the Singing Sword and the Tears of the Moon.'

'And defeat the Goblin King!' cried Elf Girl.

Rat squeaked happily.

'What did he say?' asked Elf Girl.

'He said, "Let's go!"'

So they did.

NEXT

Follow Raven Boy and Elf Girl (and Rat) as they head out towards SCREAM SEA . . .

Fright Forest

Monster Mountains

Scream Sea

Dread Desert

Terror Town

Creepy Caves